A B C
Letters in the Library

written by
Bonnie Farmer

illustrated by
Chum McLeod

Lobster Press™

ABC Letters in the Library
Text © 2004 Bonnie Farmer
Illustrations © 2004 Chum McLeod/i2iart.com

Published in 2005 by:
Lobster Press™
1620 Sherbrooke Street West, Suites C & D
Montréal, Québec   H3H 1C9
Tel. (514) 904-1100 • Fax (514) 904-1101
www.lobsterpress.com

Publisher: Alison Fripp
Editors: Alison Fripp & Karen Li
Graphic Design & Production: Tammy Desnoyers

We acknowledge the financial support of the Government of Canada through the Book Publishing Industry Development Program (BPIDP) for our publishing activities.

The Canada Council | Le Conseil des Arts
for the Arts | du Canada

We acknowledge the support of the Canada Council for the Arts for our publishing program.

Library and Archives Canada Cataloguing in Publication

Farmer, Bonnie, 1959-
        ABC letters in the library / Bonnie Farmer ; illustrated by Chum McLeod.

ISBN 1-894222-87-3 (bound).-ISBN 1-897073-19-4 (pbk.)

        1. Libraries--Juvenile literature. 2. Alphabet books. 3. English language--Alphabet--Juvenile literature. I. McLeod, Chum II. Title.

Z665.5.F37 2004   j027   C2004-901420-X

Printed and bound in Canada.

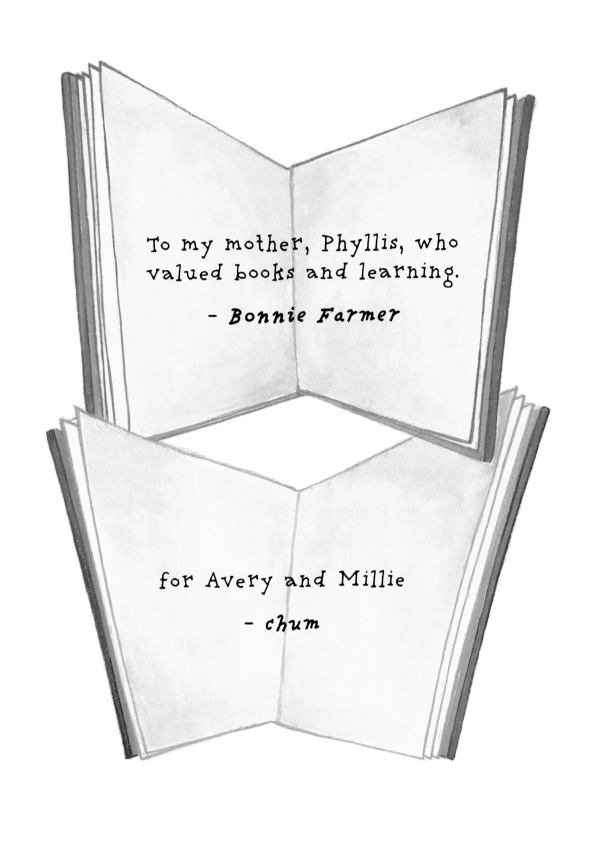

To my mother, Phyllis, who valued books and learning.

– *Bonnie Farmer*

for Avery and Millie

– *chum*

Aa

Aisles of authors
are arranged
alphabetically.

Bb

Beautiful books dazzle browsing bookworms.

Humming **c**omputers **c**ollect **c**ountless **c**all numbers.

Dense dictionaries unravel difficult terms.

Encyclopedias teach the most earnest of learners.

Ff

Fun-filled ghost stories frighten and shock.

Spinning **g**lobes
gather **g**reat dreams
of travel.

The librarian's soft *s*hhh soon hushes all talk.

Hh

Information flows freely in and out of the Internet.

A smooth glossy **j**acket
is a book's best
protection.

Kk

Searching for **k**nowledge **k**eeps **k**ids' minds wide open.

A **l**ibrarian's friendship **l**eaves **l**asting impressions.

Members view **m**aps through **m**agnifying glasses,

M **m**

While **n**appers **n**od off behind inky **n**ewspapers.

N **n**

NEWS

Overdue books keep all others waiting.

Bright **p**ages burst with eye-**p**leasing **p**ictures.

Pp

Inquisitive ones
quietly ask lots of
questions.

Qq

A reader floats off on
a soft Persian rug.

Rr

Ss

Story time spreads smiles on small students' faces.

Tt

Teachers *tsk* at loud teens,
who grin and then shrug.

Used books are
donated by
bighearted readers,

Then put into place by Valuable Volunteers.

Writers weave
wonderful
words with
their pencils.

the wizard waved his magic wand.

Young artists' e**x**hibits receive praise and cheers.

Youngsters shuffle home bearing books that they love,

And pages become pillows as stars shine above.
Zzzzzz.